First U.S. edition 2002

Library of Congress
Cataloging-in-Publication Data
is available.

Library of Congress Catalog
Card Number 2002023897

ISBN 0-7636-1901-9

Printed in Hong Kong

This book was typeset in
Garamond Book Educational.
The illustrations were done
in charcoal and watercolor.

Candlewick Press
2067 Massachusetts Avenue
Cambridge, Massachusetts 02140

visit us at www.candlewick.com

CANDLEWICK PRESS
CAMBRIDGE, MASSACHUSETTS

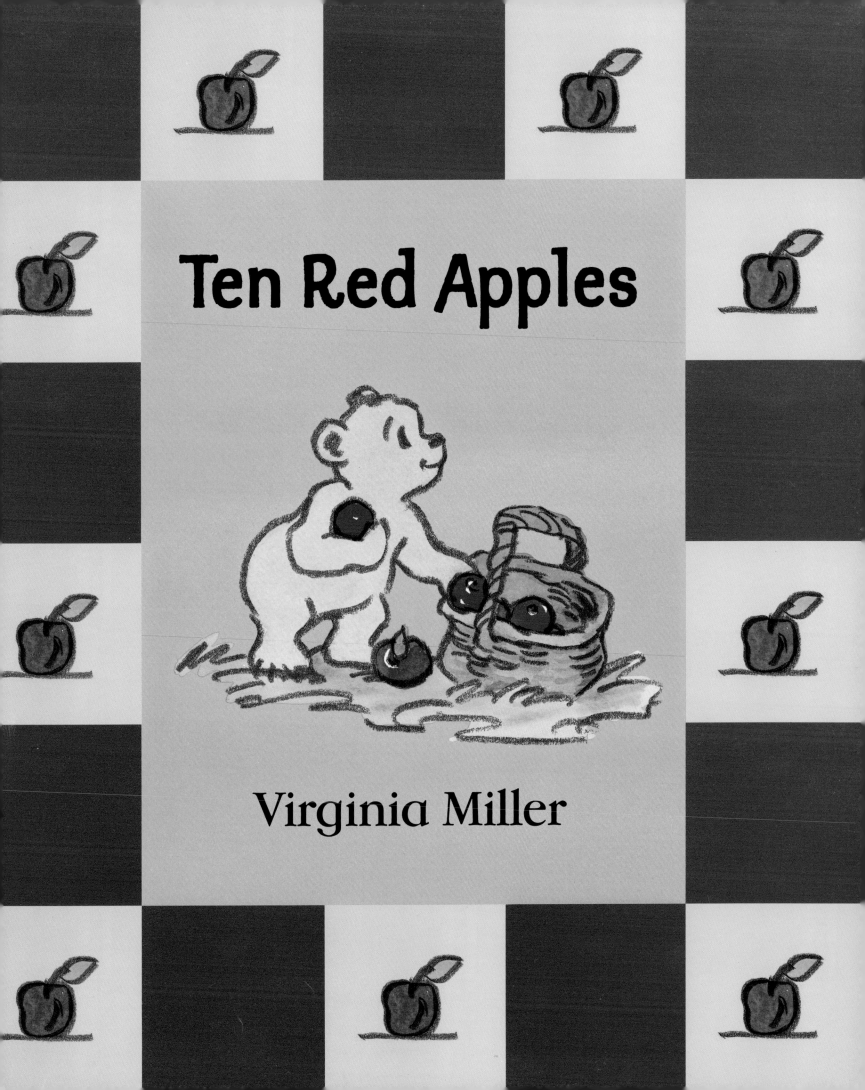

Ten Red Apples

Virginia Miller

I n Bartholomew's
garden there is
an old apple tree.

one
red apple

Bartholomew

oves the apple tree.

2

two
red apples

He love

winging from its branches,

3
three
red apples

and hugging i

ight when it rains.

4
four
red apples

He love.

limbing the tree.

5
five
red apples

When Little Blac

Kitten climbs too high . . .

six
red apples

he and Georg

have to rescue her.

7
seven
red apples

Bartholomew

oves hiding under the leaves.

8

eight
red apples

Best of all h

oves counting the red apples.

9
nine
red apples

George shake:

he apples from the tree,

10
ten
red apples

puts them

nto a basket,

0

zero
(all gone)

and makes them

nto a hot apple pie.

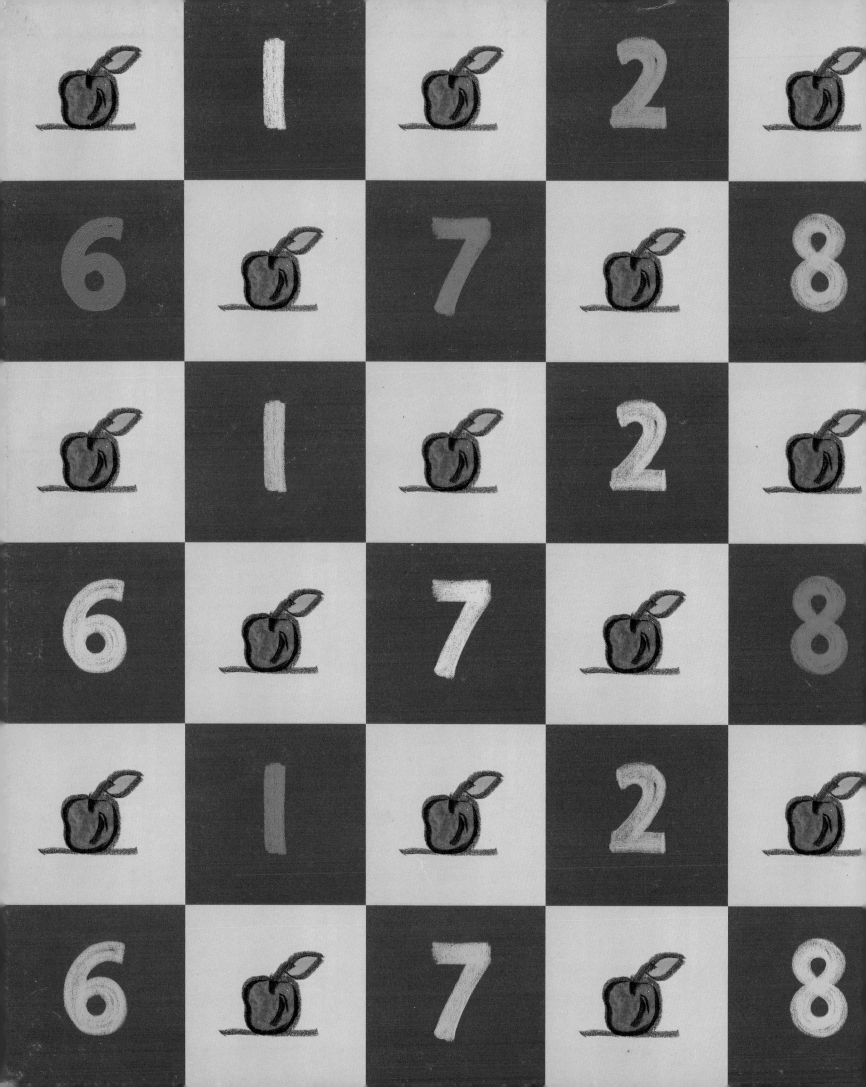